I0551531

THE POLISH DONUT

What Ben Didn't Know...

Andy Labis

Webventure Publishing

ISBN E-Book: 979-8-9945082-0-6
ISBN Paperbook: 979-8-9945082-1-3

Cover design by: Andy Labis

For my mom...

...who made paczki with no filling.

CONTENTS

A MOST GLORIOUS MORNING!

"**C**ome on, Amy! We gotta go!" Ben exclaimed as his alarm clock went off.

Rolling over to look at Ben, still tucked under the covers and wanting to sleep a little longer, Amy groggily said, "What? Why? Where?"

"It's Paczki Day!"

"What day?" asked Amy.

"Paczki Day! You know, punch-key day for you non-Polish types! We have to get going before there's a line!"

Just then Amy remembered it was Fat Tuesday, the day before Ash Wednesday. She thought back to months ago when they both scheduled this week off work, hoping to go on vacation in New Orleans for Mardi Gras. Unfortunately, the travel plans fell through, and they decided on a stay-cation instead.

"Ben, they will have plenty. We have time."

With a puzzled look of how Amy couldn't feel the same excitement he was experiencing, Ben nudged her while she tried to roll completely under the covers.

"How can you just lie there?"

Starting to get annoyed, Amy replied, "Because it's our vacation, remember, and even though it's more of a stay-cation, I want to sleep in."

"Fine," Ben snapped back like a child who wasn't getting his way, "I'll let you sleep a little longer. Is half an hour enough?"

"How about an hour?" negotiated Amy.

Ben, knowing this was a battle he was not going to win, and as he didn't want to risk having to go to the bakery alone, caved, "Okay, I'll go have some coffee."

Amy rolled back over, realizing that in exactly 60 minutes, and not a minute later, Ben would be back in the bedroom to wake her.

As Amy was drifting off for a 60-minute snooze, Ben softly started singing a haphazard tune while he was leaving the bedroom:

"It's Paczki Day

"It's Paczki Day

"Everybody say "Yay" for Paczki Day!

"No it's not a jelly donut, at least not the real ones.

"Nope, it's Paczki Day!

"It's Paczki Day

"Everybody say "Yay" for Paczki Day!"

Ben closed the door, and as he was walking down the hallway Amy could still hear him,

"It's Paczki Day,

"It's Paczki Day

"Everybody say "Yay" for Paczki Day!"

A grin came to Amy's face as she fell back asleep humming Ben's tune.

NO JELLY

As Ben was making espresso, humming his song, and a little annoyed that Amy didn't seem to share in his excitement, his thoughts took him back to his childhood memories of paczki.

The interesting thing to him, as he recalled, was that the versions that his mom made were nothing like the giant, dough balls stuffed with filling that he was now used to eating on Fat Tuesday.

He remembered his mom bringing out the pot that she usually used for making chicken soup. Ben was always amazed at the size of the pot, and the fact she could fit the entire chicken carcass in it. For paczki, though, he could envision her dumping what seemed like ten gallons of oil in the pot from the yellow, plastic bottles.

What fascinated him most, however, was the giant mercury thermometer she would clamp on the inside of the pot to make sure the oil temperature was just right.

His mom would make dough balls which were roughly the size of a tennis ball, cook them in the oil, scoop them out, and put them on weathered, metal cooling racks with paper towels underneath to catch any oil that might drip off the balls of dough.

When the balls cooled, his mom would pull out the flour sifter that never looked completely clean. The canister portion looked like an old can that might have been used to hold tomato sauce. It had a grip attached with a handle that, when squeezed, would spin the metal agitator at the bottom of the sifter, scraping along the metal screen and releasing whatever was being sifted.

Ben remembered how happy he would get when his mom would let him put the powdered sugar on the paczki. His little hand would stretch as far as it could, grabbing the grip and pulling the handle open and closed to let the powdered sugar come out of the bottom.

"That crunchy feeling of the agitator against the screen was so cool," Ben thought.

For all of his life these were the paczki that Ben knew, small, oily, dough balls with powdered sugar on them and no filling.

Thinking through more of his paczki history, Ben fast-forwarded his thoughts to being in college, and his first Fat Tuesday in Chicago. He was missing his mom's paczki, but a friend brought a box to his room. Ben opened the box and didn't understand why they were so big. He also wondered why there was filling inside of them. Finally, as he tried one, the dough and outside of the donut tasted nothing like the versions his mom made.

He remembered saying something like, "These are imposters! These are just giant, jelly donuts!"

He also remembered eating them anyway.

59 MINUTES LATER

Ben had set a timer on his watch for sixty minutes immediately after he left Amy in the bedroom. While the timer counted down, following the memories about his paczki experiences, he did his best to slowly enjoy his espresso while looking at his laptop, jumping around from website to website, and at 59 minutes he made his way back to the bedroom.

"Honey, it's been an hour. Time to get up!"

Amy groggily opened her eyes, thankful for the extra hour of sleep while also knowing she will never agree to a stay-cation on Fat Tuesday again.

"Did I ever tell you about how my mom's paczki were smaller and didn't have filling?"

Amy replied, "Yes, Honey, every Fat Tuesday since we met."

"Oh, yea," Ben answered back, seeming surprised he had told her.

"Well, I still kind of miss those. Don't get me wrong, the ones at The Garden Bakery are good and all, but there was just something about getting the powdered sugar all over the place. And that oily dough! So good!"

Amy resigned herself to the fact that for the next hour or so, and probably into the next day with the extras Ben would buy, she would be hearing about paczki, how they weren't like the ones Ben's mom would make, and how he should have bought another raspberry filled paczki instead of trying the rose flavor once again.

As they were getting ready to go to the bakery, Amy grinned at how happy Ben was. She did love how little things, like a donut, would bring a smile to Ben's face. She could, however, do without the same story every year.

Ben finished getting ready like his life depended on it, and Amy could see how impatient he was to get to the bakery.

"I hope they don't run out. I'm worried the line is going to be long," Ben mumbled under his breath, just loud enough for Amy to hear.

"They will have plenty. Don't worry. We missed the early rush, anyway," Amy commented.

"You're probably right," Ben softly said, but Amy could still hear the impatience in his voice.

"Can you please get my coat?" Amy asked.

Ben took off, almost running to the closet, getting Amy's coat and setting her shoes near the bench by the door.

Amy came around, saw the shoes, and just shook her head. They both started towards the garage once Amy had her shoes on, and Ben starting singing:

"It's Paczki Day

"It's Paczki Day

"Everybody say "Yay" for Paczki Day!

"No it's not a jelly donut, at least not the real ones.

"Nope, it's Paczki Day!

"It's Paczki Day

"Everybody say "Yay" for Paczki Day!"

Amy started humming along as they got in the car.

A SHORT WAIT

The Garden Bakery was about a twenty-minute drive from Ben and Amy's house. It wasn't the preferred place Ben would have gotten paczki, that would have been Stanislaw's Bakery and Deli which is closer to his office. Ben liked Stanislaw's because the dough seemed more authentic, and even with the filling, reminded him of the versions his mom would make. Today, however, The Garden Bakery would satisfy Ben's desire for paczki.

As they turned the corner, Ben could see the line out the door. At first he was perturbed they arrived so late, but then he remembered that the inside of the bakery was small, and most of the time the line was out the door.

Amy turned into the parking lot of the strip mall, found a spot near the bakery, and Ben jumped out like a kid running to a candy store, getting in line before Amy closed and locked the car.

There wasn't a need for Ben to go that fast as no one else was arriving, but Ben didn't want to risk it.

As they claimed their spot in line, Ben peered through the windows that looked like they hadn't been cleaned in about five years. In the front window was a myriad of nicknacks, from cookie jars to antique baking utensils. In the corner was a sifter that looked a lot like the one his mom used.

A sigh of relief came to Ben's face as he looked to the racks of baked goods behind the counter, and he saw they still had the full contingent of paczki. He counted how many people were in front of him, noting ten people, so unless a few of them decided to stock up on dozens, Ben was confident he would be able to get a raspberry version and maybe two more.

Ben noticed the man in front of them. He was dressed in clothes that looked like they came right out of the hamper, and his hair looked like it hadn't been washed in a few days. There was an anxiousness in the man's demeanor, but Ben didn't notice it right away.

Ben whispered to Amy, "See, he didn't wait to shower or worry about what to wear."

Amy sneered at Ben, patiently waiting for the line to move.

Even though Ben was preoccupied contemplating his order, wavering between different flavors in his head, even though, at the end of it all, he would end up getting the same ones he always did, he eventually noticed that the man kept looking at his watch.

"Guess he's in a hurry, too," Ben whispered to Amy.

Amy wasn't paying attention to the man up until that moment, but even she took note of the wrinkled clothes and disheveled look.

She whispered to Ben with a smile, "I guess he wanted his paczki more than you did this morning," hinting to Ben that he could have just driven himself to the bakery.

As the line kept moving, Amy and Ben were in the door, and the smell of fresh, baked goods filled Ben's nose.

Ben inhaled deeply and smiled.

THE GARDEN BAKERY

Safely inside The Garden Bakery, Ben looked around to see if anything had changed since the last time he was there a few months ago. He remembered they used to have a chime that would ring when people would walk in, but that seemed to be gone. Behind the counter was the owner, Linda. She had been there for as long as Ben could remember, but never seemed like she really wanted to be there. Coming out from the back kitchen was Greg, covered in a variety of powder and cream, almost like the toppings exploded while he was getting the donuts and pastries together.

The walls were covered in flower-print wallpaper that looked to have been there since the 1970s, and the customer area didn't look like any improvements had been made since the place opened.

The line of customers came through the door and snaked along the wall opposite the counter, then wrapped first near the case with coffee cakes, finally snaking back to the main counter area. The front counter was filled with assorted donuts and cookies, including Ben's favorites, a raised, glazed donut and a chocolate triangle, which was a raised donut in the shape of a triangle, filled with angel cream, and topped with chocolate frosting.

Normally Ben's favorite donuts were in the racks behind the counter, but with it being Fat Tuesday, those racks were filled with assorted paczki.

The back racks looked as old as the bakery, and the peeling, powder-blue paint on the wood shelving revealed that there had never been any other layers of paint since the place opened. The racks were haphazardly resting on the shelving, at a slight angle so the customers could see what was available.

Off to the side, behind the counter, rested a cash register that looked weathered but served its purpose. The plastic sides of the register, which at one time were bright white, had faded into a flat yellow, and the register spit out a receipt that was never legible as the ink probably hadn't been changed in years.

On normal days, The Garden Bakery was filled with regulars, picking up donuts for family or work, or as in Ben's case, just for themself. As Ben was standing along the wall, he remembered a time he would stop every Friday, and sometimes on Tuesday, Wednesday, or Thursday, and get his raised glaze and chocolate triangle. Linda or Greg would see him coming from the parking lot, and they would have the donuts ready for him by the time he got to the counter.

There was never much chit-chat for Ben; he just wanted his donuts, but he always did his best to be upbeat with a big smile, hoping Linda might actually smile.

Today, though, the bakery was filled with about 50% regulars and 50% people who were just there for the paczki. You could see the regulars, like Ben, were annoyed with the newcomers, but the regulars all knew that this event and annoyance only came once a year.

Ben made his way along the wall, gazing at the racks behind the counter, completely oblivious to his normal choices of donut.

Ben hummed under his breath,

"It's Paczki Day

"It's Paczki Day

"Everybody say "Yay" for Paczki Day!"

THE LINE

As the line moved forward and people started to get to the counter, Ben drifted from studying the paczki in the racks to checking out the customers ahead of him. While the inside of the bakery was small and normally sparsely filled with people, on Fat Tuesday the floor was packed with customers from five to eighty-five years old. Also, since it was just Linda helping the customers, it would sometimes take a while for the line to move along.

At the front of the line was a family of four, and they were taking a while to make up their minds, mostly because the five-year-old and eight-year-old were completely overwhelmed by the choices.

Ben could overhear the mother, "They have raspberry, strawberry, custard, plum, and rose."

"What's rose?" inquired the eight-year-old girl, "Is that like eating roses?"

"It has that flavor," mentioned the mother.

"Ewww, I would be eating a flower?"

Ben chuckled a little bit hearing this because that was always his thought.

"No, you wouldn't be eating a flower, but you know how a rose smells beautiful? It would taste like that smell," the mother tried to explain.

"I do like the smell of flowers. Can I get a rose one?"

Ben knew the child would not be happy with her choice.

Behind the family was an older couple whom Ben had seen a few times in the bakery. The wife seemed mesmerized with the family in front of them while Ben could see the husband eying the rack of strawberry paczki, sometimes drifting his gaze to the case filled with donuts, then turning to the side to look at the coffee cakes. Ben knew what was coming when the couple had their chance to order.

The family of four made their decisions, and Ben overheard their order: Three raspberry, two strawberry, two custard, and a rose. Ben figured that at least half of the rose paczki would end up in the garbage.

As the older couple made their way to the counter, Ben knew this order would be quick. The woman greeted Linda, "Hi Linda! Busy morning?"

"Yea, always is. What can I get you?" asked Linda wearily, as if wondering if the line would ever end.

"I'll just have one raspberry. Charlie, tell Linda what flavor you want."

Charlie's head spun around the bakery shop. "I'll have a strawberry and a cherry one. And can you add a chocolate-covered long-john? And, will the coffee cake last through the weekend?"

Linda looked flustered, "It will probably just make it."

The woman started shaking her head, "Charlie, that's too much."

"I'll also take an almond coffee cake."

"Ugh," exclaimed the wife.

Linda looked annoyed at having to go over to the coffee cake counter. She put the pastry in a bag perfectly shaped for coffee cakes, and then stacked the paczki in a small box.

The couple made their way to the register with Linda, and the disheveled man in front of Ben and Amy was next in line.

Ben noticed the man looked nervous and seemed to be in a hurry, but he also had a look of knowing exactly what he wanted. This brought a slight sense of relief to Ben, knowing he would be able to get his paczki soon. Ben went back to scanning his choices. Even though The Garden Bakery only had five varieties of paczki, he was generally frozen trying to decide.

"Hi, I'm Phil," said the man to Linda. Linda seemed to not care.

"What can I get you?" asked Linda.

Phil thought for the briefest of moments, "Can I get one raspberry and one plum?"

Ben, overhearing the choice of plum, thought, "Eww. I guess he's that guy who buys the plum flavor."

As Linda turned around, grabbing the wax paper and then the two paczki, she asked Phil, "Is a bag okay?"

"A bag will be fine."

Linda led Phil over to the register, but Amy noticed panic come over Phil as he reached to his back pocket and discovered his wallet wasn't there.

As Phil got to the register area, Amy could hear Phil, with a quiver in his voice as if he might cry, "Is there any way I can take them and come back with the money. I forgot my wallet."

Linda replied, "We have plenty. You can just come back, and we'll probably still have some."

"You don't understand, I don't have a lot of time," as tears started coming to Phil's eyes.

Linda seemed agitated and said, "I'm sorry you forgot your wallet, but you can come back."

While Amy was paying attention to the interaction between

Phil and Linda, Ben was oblivious to what was happening at the register, still unsure of what his choices might be.

Phil had a look of being both crestfallen and despondent that he had forgotten his wallet. Meanwhile, Linda, growing impatient, started to make the motion of taking the paczki out of the bag to put them back on the shelf.

Amy walked over to the register, "I'll pay for his. How much is it?"

"$5.50," replied Linda.

As Amy handed Linda her credit card, Phil had a look of stunned relief and gratitude saying to Amy, "Oh my God. God bless you. Thank you. You have no idea how much this means to me. I'll pay you back. Can you let me know how I can contact you?"

Amy replied with comfort in her voice, seeming to understand that, for some reason, these two paczki meant the world to the man, "It's Fat Tuesday, enjoy!"

Ben noticed Amy paying for Phil's order. He seemed inquisitive at what had happened, but was more concerned with his upcoming choices.

With Phil being done with his order, Linda came over to Ben.

"Hi, what can I get you?"

"I'll take a raspberry and a rose. Can you also add a chocolate triangle?" Ben then turned to Amy, "Honey, tell Linda what you want."

Amy shook her head, knowing Ben ordered too many items and would complain about the rose-flavored paczki, then looked at Linda, "I'll have a raspberry."

As Amy and Ben made their way to the register, Ben asked Amy, "Did you pay for that guy's paczki?"

"Yeah, he forgot his wallet."

"Who comes to a bakery without their wallet on paczki day?" asked Ben with a sound of bewilderment.

What Ben didn't know was that Phil's mother was about to die.

PHIL

When Phil found out his mother had stage four cancer, he put his life on hold.

She had lived all of her life in a suburb of Chicago, while years ago Phil had moved to the west coast for work. The move was a challenge for Phil, an only child, who would be what most considered a momma's boy. While not pleased about the move, it seemed like his only chance for advancement at his company.

In retrospect, the move turned out to be a mistake for Phil on many levels. His wife was never happy living out west, eventually divorcing Phil for a man she met at a gym, and the chance for the promotion was short-lived as the company decided to eliminate the position Phil was being trained for after he had already moved.

While he still kept in touch with his friends, Phil never fit in on the west coast and couldn't adjust to the lifestyle, either.

He was a midwestern boy at heart.

He also missed his mother terribly. They would talk on the phone every weekend, and whenever she would bring up something she needed done, whether as simple as a light bulb which needed replacing, or as complicated as when her landscaper didn't show up to mow the grass, Phil felt it was his fault that his mother was having these troubles. It killed him that he couldn't be there to help.

Putting his life on hold, though, became Phil's number one priority knowing that his mother only had about one more year to live following the diagnosis.

It had been nearly a year that Phil had quit his job to move back and live with his mother. While he was thinking about things on this Fat Tuesday morning, he realized that he didn't miss the job at all. He thought back to how the company screwed him over by making him move out to the west coast for the position they ended up eliminating. He was also happy that he had been frugal enough to save enough money so that quitting work for a few years wasn't an issue. As his mother had no one around any longer, Phil knew he couldn't just leave her in the midwest to die on her own.

Through that year Phil had seen his mother's health get worse and worse. While she started with the standard course of treatment for her cancer, the doctors suggested she try a new treatment that was supposed to give her another six months to a year to live. The side effects, however, were excruciating, and while Phil wanted her to continue, being afraid to lose her, his mother decided she had enough. She felt it was her time, and it wasn't worth it to live six more months being completely miserable.

They both decided home hospice was how her end would come.

The days blended together, and as things progressed, some days were worse than others, but lately the worse days began outnumbering the better. The hospice nurse had made his weekly visit the day before Fat Tuesday and told Phil that he didn't think Phil's mom would be alert more than one more day, and probably pass away in the next day or two. While mentally Phil had been planning this for the past year, hearing it was like a punch to the gut. The nurse also mentioned that Phil's mother shouldn't be left alone these last few days. In her state she might try to walk on her own, or might fall, or even just fall out of her chair.

Phil acknowledged this wouldn't be a problem, that he didn't need to go anywhere for at least a week to pick up any food or supplies.

TORN

As Phil checked on his mother on Fat Tuesday morning, she was more cognizant than he had seen her in days, even turning on the morning news. There was a story about the line at a local bakery for Fat Tuesday, everyone getting paczki, and Phil's mother said in a remarkably cheery voice upon seeing Phil, "Good morning son! It's Fat Tuesday! Remember when I would make you paczki?"

"Yes, mom. I always liked yours even though they didn't have any filling."

"That's the way I was taught to make them, but I always did like those ones with plum filling that you used to buy me," commented his mother.

Then she asked, "Do you think you could run to the bakery and get me one?"

Phil was torn. He was told his mother shouldn't be left alone, and he had no one he could call to come over to watch her for a short period of time.

"Mom, you know you aren't supposed to be left alone," said Phil with disappointment.

"Oh, okay," said Phil's mother, in a voice that crushed Phil's soul knowing this might be the last treat she would ever get.

Phil tried to think of anyone he might be able to ask to watch his mother, but he had never made friends with any of the new neighbors, and was pretty sure he had seen all of them already leave their houses.

As he sat in the living room for a few minutes, watching the TV with her and seeing another news story of a bakery with people standing in line to get paczki, he decided at that minute he had to take the chance.

Phil rushed to his bedroom, quickly changed into some day-old jeans, threw on the first t-shirt he could find, grabbed his car keys, and hurried back to the living room not realizing that his wallet had fallen out of his jeans as he was putting them on.

With nervousness in his voice, Phil said, "Mom, I'm going to run out for a few minutes and get us paczki. Can you promise that you won't do anything, won't get up, and will just stay in your chair and watch T.V.? Maybe you'll see me in line!"

Phil knew he was going to be at a different bakery, but hoped that by telling her to watch for him, she wouldn't get out of her chair while he was gone.

"Oh, that sounds like fun. Don't worry, Philly, I'll stay right here. Hurry back!" exclaimed his mother.

Phil gave his mom a kiss and hurried to his car feeling completely distraught at having to leave her alone, but knowing that he couldn't live with himself if he didn't go and get her one, last, plum paczki.

As he drove to The Garden Bakery, he felt lucky, making every green light, and thought maybe this was a sign from God that he was doing the right thing. That thought quickly changed when he got to the bakery and saw the line out the door.

Taking his place in line, he hoped things would move quickly. To try to take his mind off of things, he took out his phone and started scrolling social media. In his feed were the standard birthday wishes, advertisements that made him wonder how they knew he was going to be looking to move soon, and then he saw a headline that read, "Click to Find the New Way the Government is Fighting Climate Change."

Phil clicked to get to the story and was surprised to find, "In the latest government study, they have decided to try and airdrop an army of environmentally conscious otters into Lake Michigan to fight Asian Carp and combat climate change."

Phil shook his head and put his phone back into his pocket realizing the link was just some fake news story. He was also oblivious to Ben and Amy who had taken their place in line behind him.

All he could do in line was fidget while trying to think of anything but his mother sitting alone, in front of her TV, watching for him on the news.

Finally he made his way to the front of the line.

"Hi, I'm Phil"

"What can I get you?"

"Can I get one raspberry and one plum?"

"Is a bag okay?"

"A bag will be fine."

"Is there any way I can take them and come back with the money. I forgot my wallet."

"We have plenty. You can just come back and we'll probably still have some."

"You don't understand, I don't have a lot of time."

"I'm sorry you forgot your wallet, but you can come back."

"I'll pay for his. How much is it?"

"$5.50."

"Oh my God. God bless you. Thank you. You have no idea how much this means to me. I'll pay you back. Can you let me know how I can contact you?"

"It's Fat Tuesday, enjoy!"

Phil took the bag of paczki and hurried back to his car, catching all green lights on the drive back home.

As he came in the door, he was relieved to hear, "Philly, is that you? I didn't see you on the TV."

He made his way to the living room, "Yea, mom, I guess they were facing a different way when I got there. I got the paczki."

Phil went back to the kitchen and put each of the paczki on plates, returned to the living room, and gave his mother the plate with the plum paczki.

She coughed a little bit, and the powdered sugar exploded like a dust cloud, covering her shirt and pants. Seeing this made Phil laugh as he was just getting ready to eat his raspberry version, causing a cascade of powdered sugar down the front of his clothes.

His mother laughed, and they both sat, saying nothing, eating their paczki while lovingly gazing at each other.

When they finished Phil got up to get her plate, "Is there anything else you need, mommy."

"I'm okay, Philly. Thank you for getting the paczki. It was just what I needed."

Phil took their plates to the kitchen, cleaned them off, and upon returning to the living room caught his mom's eyes beginning to close. As she looked at him, an ever so small smile came to her face. She whispered, "Don't worry, I'm okay," and her eyes closed.

That was the last time Phil would see his mother's eyes.

CAN'T WAIT

As they were going to their car, it was one of the many times Ben was happy that Amy didn't like his driving. Ben raced to the car, waiting impatiently for Amy to unlock the doors. Climbing in, Ben tried to navigate buckling his seat belt while opening the box of goodies.

The bakery tape was the first challenge.

"Honey, whoever invented this tape that bakeries use should be fired. I shouldn't need a knife to cut open this tape."

As Ben tried to tear the tape, he realized it would be easier to try to peel it off of the box. Unfortunately his nails only caught a corner of the tape, pulling half of it, leaving the other half to keep the box securely sealed.

"Ugh!" Ben exclaimed.

Amy said, "Honey, give me the box."

Ben begrudgingly gave Amy the box knowing she had the magic touch, and in a matter of seconds Amy returned the opened box to Ben.

He opened the lid like a kid opening his present on Christmas morning, revealing the variety of paczki inside, and one donut.

"I can't believe I didn't get a coffee cake, too," said Ben.

Amy shook her head.

"Hmm? Which one to have?" asked Ben.

Amy replied, "Can't you wait until we get home, you're going to get powdered sugar all over my car."

"I'll be careful. I'm a trained, paczki-eating professional!" proclaimed Ben.

Amy shook her head again.

Amy started the drive home, and Ben took out one of the two raspberry paczki from the box. As he started to bring it to his mouth, he took a small breath, inhaling some powdered sugar. This caused Ben to sneeze, and as much as he tried to move his mouth away from the paczki, he wasn't quick enough, and a cloud of powdered sugar drifted in the direction of the car's dashboard.

"Don't worry, I'll clean that up," said Ben, with a look of resignation at what was coming next.

"What was that you said?" asked Amy, "Something like, 'Trained, paczki-eating professional?'"

Ben grinned as he finally took a bite of his paczki, smiling with delight, finishing it before they made it home.

As they got to the kitchen, Ben made a latte for each of them, and went back to the pastry box.

"That's your raspberry, isn't it?" he asked Amy.

"Yes. I wouldn't buy a rose paczki," mentioned Amy with a slight hint of "I could have told you so."

Ben handed the raspberry one to Amy, grabbed the rose paczki out of the box, and took a bite of it.

"Why do I buy one every year thinking I'm going to like it? Oh well, glad I bought the donut!" said Ben.

As he tossed the rest of the rose paczki in the garbage, he smiled from ear to ear as he took a giant bite of the triangle donut.

STANISLAW'S BAKERY

A few weeks later, while driving to work, Ben was thinking back to Fat Tuesday, and his mistake of getting the rose paczki.

"Why do they only have paczki on Fat Tuesday? Oh, wait, that's right, The Garden Bakery only has them on Fat Tuesday."

Getting to the traffic light, he looked at the clock on his dashboard, "Dang, I'll be late if I try to swing by the bakery," he thought.

"I know, no one will care if I come with a box of paczki for the office!"

Ben made a right turn instead of going straight, arriving at Stanislaw's Bakery and Deli. He could see the deli counter at the back of the store, but it had yet to be stocked with various Polish dishes.

"I wonder why I never come in here for lunch? I could go for a good stuffed cabbage or potato pancake."

He made his way to the register where there were trays of paczki in all flavors, and he could tell from the oil on the wax paper on the trays that these were more traditional than those at The Garden Bakery.

A man was ahead of him in line.

"Can I have one raspberry and one plum?"

The woman behind the counter put the two paczki in a bag, and as the man passed him, Ben thought, "I don't know why, but that guy looks familiar."

Ben took his spot at the counter and asked, "Can I get a dozen paczki, please?"

In a broken, English accent the woman said, "Any flavor?"

"A mix is fine. And can you put two raspberry in a separate bag?" replied Ben.

The woman commented, "You should get two different flavor. The rose is very good."

A sudden feeling of needing to please the bakery owner came over Ben as he grudgingly responded, "Okay, one raspberry and one rose."

Ben paid for his order feeling better knowing that while he might be late to work, no one would judge him since he brought the paczki. He was also going to be able to explain, as he often did, that you can get paczki all year round if you go to a Polish bakery.

He made his way to his car, opened up his special stash in the separate bag, bit into the rose paczki, and shook his head in his own bewilderment, "Why did I get a rose one again?"

Ben swapped out the rose one for the raspberry paczki which was still in the bag and began to eat the raspberry version. He inhaled while taking a bite, proceeded to sneeze, and powdered sugar sprayed all over his shirt, steering wheel, and dashboard.

Meanwhile, as Ben was eating his paczki in the car, Phil had already pulled out of the bakery parking lot thinking, "That guy looked familiar."

Phil's destination was a few miles away. He continued down the street, with his bag of a raspberry and plum paczki resting on the passenger seat, and saw his destination up ahead. He made a turn and drove through the wrought-iron archway that framed the entrance, continuing down the well-manicured, tree-lined road.

He pulled over to the side and got a blanket from the back seat.

With the sun shining through the trees, Phil made his way to the clearing, watching carefully where he was walking. Arriving at his spot, he laid out the blanket just to the side of a headstone which read, "Loving wife and mother."

Phil took the paczki out of the bag, put the plum paczki on the top of the headstone, and sat down on the blanket. He brought the raspberry paczki near his mouth and said, "This is for you, mom."

As he went to take a bite of his paczki, he accidentally breathed in some powdered sugar. A sneeze erupted, and as the cloud of powdered sugar covered the front of his clothes, Phil smiled as a tear ran down his cheek.

MOM'S PACZKI RECIPE

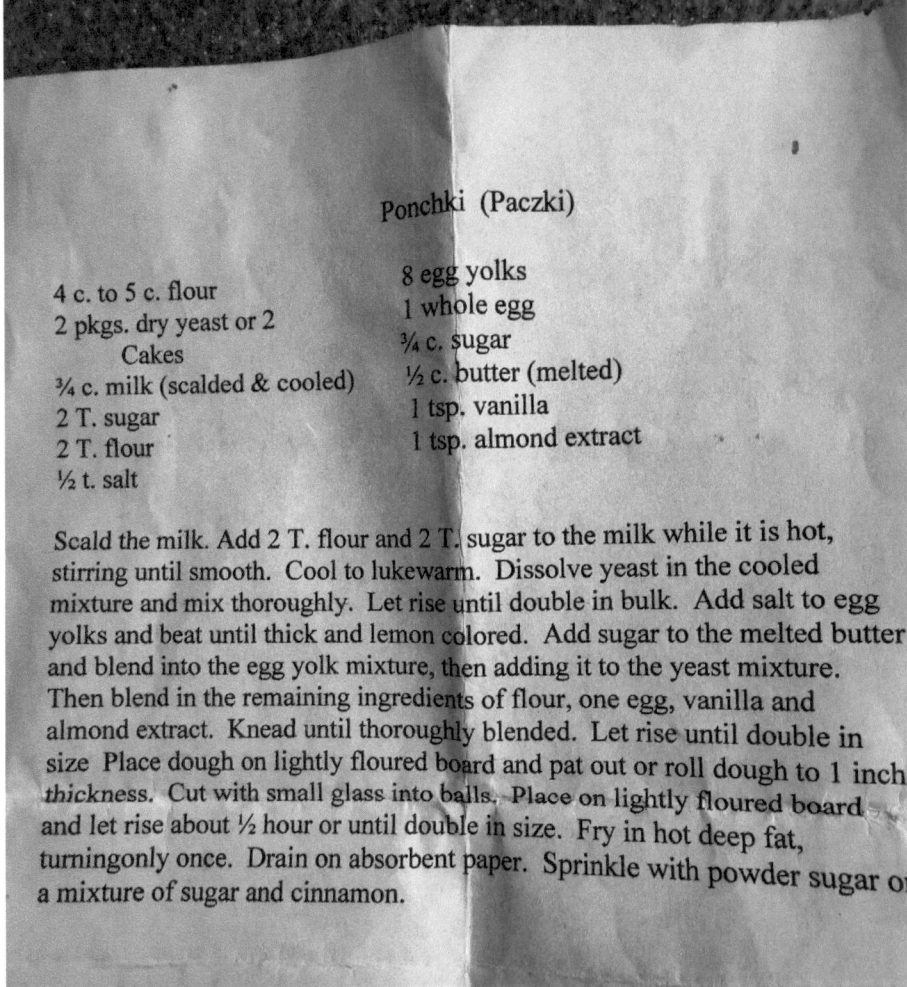

Ponchki (Paczki)

4 c. to 5 c. flour
2 pkgs. dry yeast or 2
    Cakes
¾ c. milk (scalded & cooled)
2 T. sugar
2 T. flour
½ t. salt

8 egg yolks
1 whole egg
¾ c. sugar
½ c. butter (melted)
1 tsp. vanilla
1 tsp. almond extract

Scald the milk. Add 2 T. flour and 2 T. sugar to the milk while it is hot, stirring until smooth. Cool to lukewarm. Dissolve yeast in the cooled mixture and mix thoroughly. Let rise until double in bulk. Add salt to egg yolks and beat until thick and lemon colored. Add sugar to the melted butter and blend into the egg yolk mixture, then adding it to the yeast mixture. Then blend in the remaining ingredients of flour, one egg, vanilla and almond extract. Knead until thoroughly blended. Let rise until double in size Place dough on lightly floured board and pat out or roll dough to 1 inch thickness. Cut with small glass into balls. Place on lightly floured board and let rise about ½ hour or until double in size. Fry in hot deep fat, turningonly once. Drain on absorbent paper. Sprinkle with powder sugar or a mixture of sugar and cinnamon.

CONNECTING

To stay connected to Ben and his adventures:
www.whatbendidntknow.com

To stay connected with the author, Andy:
www.allthingsandy.com

For images from Ben's adventures:
www.imagebyandy.store/collections/ben

ACKNOWLEDGEMENT

As I continue the "What Ben Didn't Know..." series, I remain deeply grateful for the support of family, friends, and readers. Your encouragement keeps me excited to continue sharing Ben's journeys.

For "The Polish Donut," I'd especially like to thank Sam McAdams from the Illinois Novel Quest group. During a writing session challenge, participants had to work a random phrase into their story to win a small momento. Mine was: "Airdrop an army of environmentally conscious otters into Lake Michigan to fight Asian Carp and combat climate change." Finding a way to fit that into the story was half the fun - and I won a writing buddy. Thanks, Sam!

Just Another Lunchtime Walk

Ben feels the need to get out of the workplace during his lunch break, and when the weather is nice, he likes to take a walk in a nearby park. As fate would have it, on this day, Laura, who lives near the park, decides to go for a walk at the same time Ben is finishing up his lunchtime walk.

The Coffee Journey

As summer fades into autumn's gray embrace, Ben discovers a new sanctuary for his lunch breaks: a cozy local coffee shop. But today, he's running late.

Miranda, a college student, finds herself at the same café earlier than usual, seeking a break from her studies.

When an unexpected delay in Ben's order leads to a simple act of kindness, it sets off a chain reaction that touches Miranda's life in a way she couldn't have anticipated.

The Driver

Ben's commute to his downtown office takes an unexpected turn. After a commuter train ride, he is forced to use a ride-sharing service due to unexpected rain and a forgotten umbrella.

His driver, Richard, proves to be more than Ben bargained for, filling the journey with uncomfortable conversation and a few close calls on the road.

ABOUT THE AUTHOR

Andy Labis

Andy Labis writes heartwarming, quietly surprising short stories about ordinary moments that change everything for people like Ben and the strangers Ben meets. His fiction lingers in the small details that reveal how connection, kindness, and paying attention can reshape a life.

Drawing on a love of photography and nature, Andy brings a visual, grounded sensibility to his storytelling.When he's not writing, he's usually behind a camera, out on a trail, or planning a new adventure, collecting the real-life textures that find their way into his work.

To learn more about Andy visit:
  www.allthingsandy.com

For more adventures in Ben's world, visit:
  www.whatbendidntknow.com

www.ingramcontent.com/pod-product-compliance
Lightning Source LLC
Chambersburg PA
CBHW040900120626
46551CB00001B/96